The Day the Holidays Blew Away

written by Maureen Llewellyn

illustrated by Olga Kutuzova

To George and Peg for encouraging
me to climb every mountain.
To Tom, Abby and Katie for believing
in me enough to try, and to Jen for that
final push...I am grateful to all of you!
Go raibh mile maith agat!

M.L.

StoryBook GENIUS PUBLISHING
sbgpublishing.com

Book Design by yipjar.com

It happened long ago on one most fateful day,
that a big wind came and blew...

Calendar's months away!

Calendar was very upset and he wanted to cry
as he watched his months fly off into the big blue sky.

"Don't cry my friend," yelled Les the Leprechaun.

"I will do my best to hold on..."

"To my regret, I could not hold on and Calender's months are now all gone! The month of March, which leprechauns hold dear, is now far away and not very near! So I'm off to find St. Patrick's Day and hope my cheer will light the way!"

A holiday of love was the first that Les did find...
but love was not the emotion felt, nor was it on his mind.

Cupid's arrows filled many hearts with pleasure, except
for our dear Les's heart, which ached for an Irish treasure!

"February is not the month that celebrates my Irish holiday, but I will collect this one for safe return once I find my day!"

Next Les came upon a holiday with bunnies big and tall
and colored baskets filled with eggs in sizes big and small!

"This is definitely not my holiday!
Bunnies and eggs are not
the good ol' Irish way."

Les came upon another month with trees full of color and Native Americans and pilgrims sat down and shared a supper.

"Oh no! Not again, I've certainly gone astray.
I fear I'll never find the route to my St. Patrick's Day!"

A cold month came upon Les next, filled with Christmas cheer and a big old happy Santa with a belly and a beard!

Les again did realize that this was not his day and hopped aboard a giant sleigh and set forth on his way.

His sleigh stopped at a celebration filled with cheer and fun.
Les saw bold fireworks exploding—brighter than the sun!

"This is a celebration of freedom—not my Irish day.
So off I go again, in hopes I find my way..."

Les came upon the month of August with hope
he had found his way, but no such luck as the
wind picked up and blew him to New Year's Day...

then to October...

then to June...

...and finally to the month of May!

"I have given it my all and searched near and far,
but St. Patrick's Day just can't be found,"
cried poor Les as he fell to the ground.

No sooner than he took a seat, and began to softly
cry, did the familiar sounds of bagpipes and
cheers put a sparkle in his eye.

Les quickly hopped up to his feet
and turned around to see...

...his favorite day filled with leprechauns, pots of gold and rainbows full of dreams! "St. Patrick's Day is **here**!" Les let out a scream.

"I am home! My heart is happy. I wish that I could stay but there's something left that I must do...so I'll be on my way!"

The luck-o-the-Irish was with him
again as he set off to see his friend!

CPSIA information can be obtained
at www.ICGtesting.com
Printed in the USA
LVHW071228050221
678464LV00011B/155

9 781952 954573